Big Brother

By Nicole Pringle

Big Brother

Written by Nicole Pringle
with Henry Charles, Jr.
Copyright © 2021 Nicole Pringle
All rights reserved.
ISBN: 978-1-7371735-0-2

DEDICATED TO
the beloved Sylvia Pringle

Jacob & Joshua Fareau

I have a new baby sister. She has tiny feet and tiny fingers.

Mom and Dad said she would grow big and strong just like me.

Mom and Dad do everything for my new baby sister.

Mom feeds my baby sister milk and baby food. Baby food looks mushy and soft. Baby food looks different from the food I like to eat.

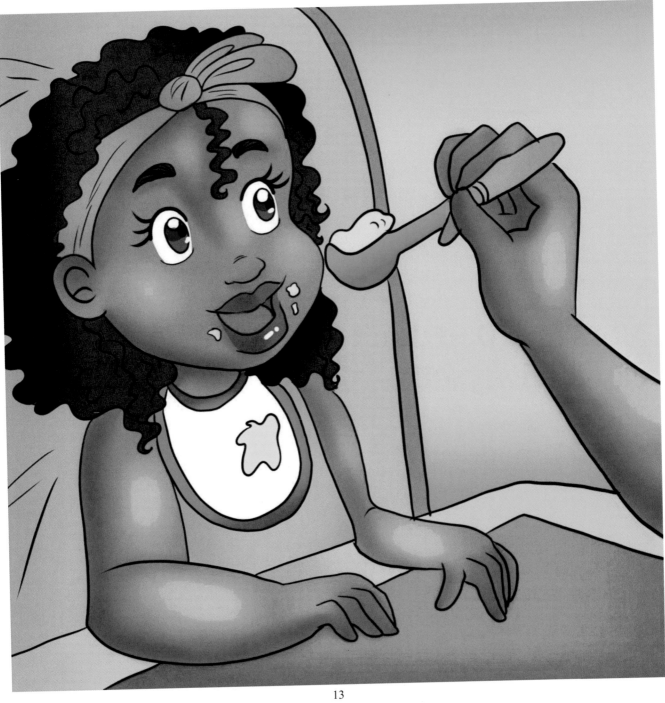

Mom and Dad don't feed me anymore. I can feed myself.

Dad changes baby sister's diapers.

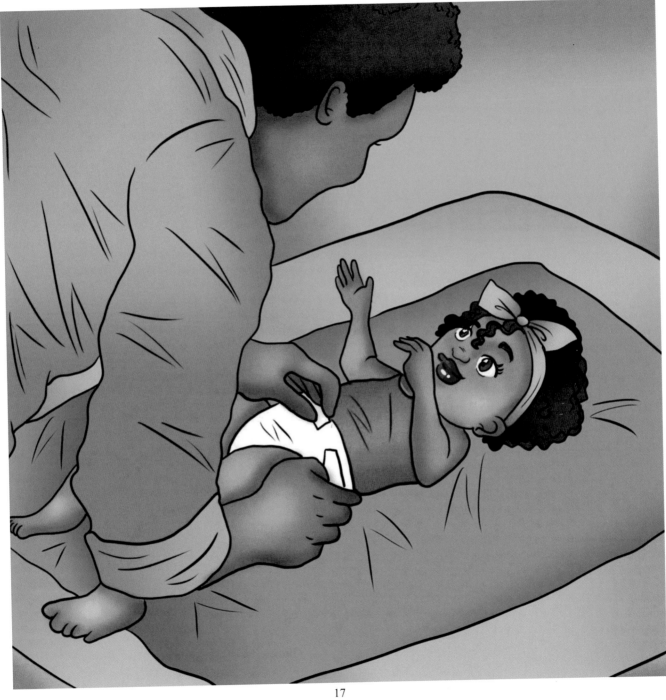

Dad doesn't help me in the bathroom. I can use the bathroom and brush my teeth all by myself.

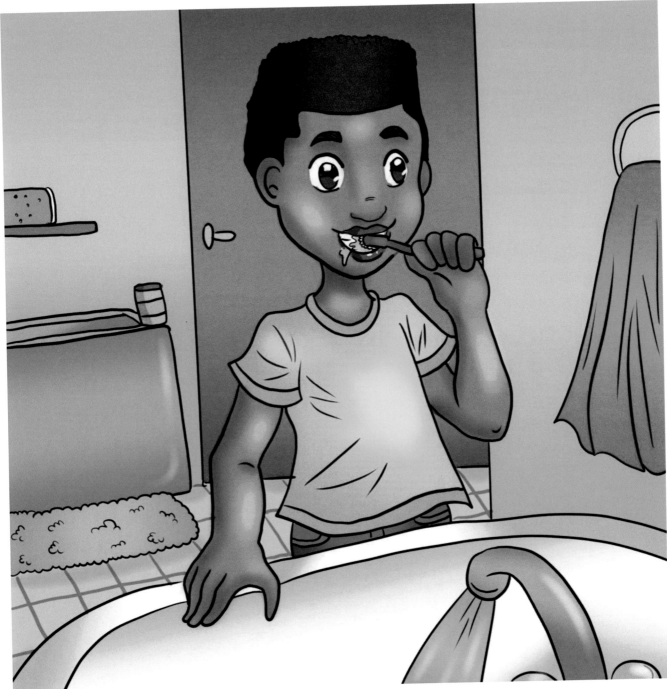

Mom gives my baby sister a bath in a little tub.

Mom doesn't help me take a bath. I can bathe all by myself.

I can do it all by myself. I am a big boy!

My baby sister loves to crawl and roll around. Mom said that is how she explores her body and soon she'll learn to walk.

Well, it turns out mom was right!

Big brother will always be here to help.

The End

About the Author

Nicole Pringle was born and raised in Brooklyn, New York and credits her seven siblings for writing this book. Nicole is a proud educator and devoted mother of two sons, Jacob and Joshua. Nicole earned a Bachelor's degree in Early Childhood Education with a concentration in Children Studies from Brooklyn College. She then earned a Master's of Science Degree in Instructional Technology (Grades K-12th) from Touro College. After earning her Masters in 2014, Nicole launched a tutor company, Tutor For Toddlers. During the COVID pandemic in 2020, Nicole has decided to relaunch her tutor company, Tutor For Toddlers LLC to provide tutor services virtually. Nicole dedicates her book to her parents, Barry and Sylvia Pringle and her children.